*In memory of my dad, Lyuba, with whom*
*I enjoyed watching thunderstorms.*

Copyright © 2000 by Manya Stojic

Published by Crown Publishers, a division of Random House, Inc., 1540 Broadway, New York, New York 10036.
Published in the United Kingdom by David Bennett Books Limited.

CROWN and colophon are trademarks of Random House, Inc.

www.randomhouse.com/kids

Printed in China

*Library of Congress Cataloging-in-Publication Data*
Stojic, Manya.
Rain / written and illustrated by Manya Stojic. — 1st American ed.
p. cm.
Summary: The animals of the African savanna use their senses to predict and then enjoy the rain.
ISBN 0-517-80085-3 (trade). — ISBN 0-517-80086-1 (lib. bdg.)
[1. Rain and rainfall—Fiction. 2. Zoology—Africa—Fiction. 3. Senses and sensation—Fiction. 4. Africa—Fiction.] I. Title.
PZ7.S873Rai 2000
[E]—dc21 99-35298

20 19 18 17 16 15 14 13 12 11

First American Edition

# Rain

## WRITTEN AND ILLUSTRATED BY
## MANYA STOJIC

Crown Publishers ♛ New York

# It was hot.
Everything was hot and dry.

The red soil was hot and dry and cracked.

A porcupine sniffed around. "It's time," she whispered. "The rain is coming! I can smell it. I must tell the zebras."

Lightning **flashed.**
" **The rain is coming!** "
said the zebras.

"Porcupine can smell it. We can SEE it. We must tell the baboons."

Thunder
boomed.

**"The rain is coming!"** cried the baboons.

**"Porcupine can smell it. The zebras can see it.**

**We can hear it. We must tell the rhino."**

A raindrop **Splashed.**

"The rain is here!"
said the rhino.

"Porcupine smelled it.
The zebras saw it.
The baboons heard it.

And I **felt** it.

I must tell the **lion.**"

The lion
spoke
in a
deep
**purr.**

"Yes, the rain is here.

I can smell it.
I can see it.
I can hear it.
I can feel it.

And," he sighed,

"I can **taste** it."

It rained until every river

gushed and gurgled.

It rained until every water hole

was full.

Then the rain stopped and everywhere long, feathery grasses grew from the soil.

Every tree began to sprout
fresh, green leaves.

"I can't taste the rain now," purred the lion,

"but I can enjoy the shade of these big, green leaves."

"I can't feel the rain now," said the rhino,

"but I can lie in the **cool, soft, squelchy mud.**"

"We can't hear the rain now," shouted the baboons,

"but we can eat

**fresh,**

**juicy fruit**

from the trees."

"We can't see the rain now," said the zebras,

"but we can have a **refreshing drink** from the water hole."

"I can't smell the rain now," whispered the porcupine, "but **I know** that it will come back again. When it's **time.**"

The sun shone over the plain.

It was **hot.**

Everything was drying out.

The red soil was
hot and dry.

A tiny crack appeared.